SCOOBY-DOO! AND THE TOY STORE TERROR

Look for the **Scooby-Doo Mysteries**.
Collect them all!

SCOOBY-DOO! AND THE TOY STORE TERROR

Written by
James Gelsey

WORLDWIDE PUBLISHING

A
LITTLE APPLE
PAPERBACK

SCHOLASTIC INC.
New York Toronto London Auckland Sydney
Mexico City New Delhi Hong Kong

For Karen

No part of this publication may be reproduced in whole or in part, or stored in a retrieval system, or transmitted in any form or by any means, electronic, mechanical, photocopying, recording, or otherwise, without written permission of the publisher. For information regarding permission, write to Scholastic Inc., Attention: Permissions Department, 555 Broadway, New York, NY 10012.

ISBN 0-439-18880-6

12 11 10 9 8 7 6 5 4 3 2   1 2 3 4 5 6/0

Printed in the U.S.A.
First Scholastic printing, May 2001

CARTOON NETWORK

SCOOBY-DOO!

AND THE

TOY STORE TERROR

Chapter 1

"Let's go, fellas," Velma called into the back of the van. "Time to wake up!"

Scooby slowly raised his head. "Ruh?" he said sleepily.

"Like, what time is it?" Shaggy asked.

"It's almost nine o'clock in the morning," Daphne replied.

"Nine o'clock in the morning?" Shaggy said. "That's, like, the middle of the night to me and Scooby-Doo."

"Well, it's first thing in the morning to the rest of the world," Velma said. "So rise and shine so we can make it to Fowler's Fun House before it gets too crowded."

"There's probably going to be a big crowd, so I'm going to park here," Fred said. He steered the Mystery Machine into a parking space on the street. Then he, Daphne, and Velma got out of the van and started walking down the street. Shaggy and Scooby slowly followed.

"Like, what's the big deal about going to a fun house this early in the morning?" asked Shaggy.

"It's not a fun house, Shaggy," Daphne said. "It's a toy store. And today they're introducing Calico Carly."

"Oh," replied Shaggy. "Who's Calico Carly?"

"A doll," Fred said.

"Not just any doll," Daphne corrected him. "She's the newest doll sensation, and my younger cousin wants one for her birthday.

2

Fowler's is the only store in town selling her."

"And that's why we're getting there right when they open," Velma explained. "We want to try to beat the crowds."

"It looks like we're a little late," Fred said.

The gang saw a huge crowd of people gathered in front of Fowler's Fun House. There were people of all ages waiting to go inside. A lot of the children were even dressed up like their favorite doll characters. The gang walked over and joined the crowd.

"All these people are here for a doll?" asked Shaggy. "I don't get it. Now, if they were waiting in line for pizza or something, that would be different."

"Reaking rof rizza . . ." Scooby said, rubbing his stomach.

"You're right, pal," Shaggy agreed. "Getting up so early has thrown my stomach clock way out of whack. What do you say we grab a quick breakfast?"

"We have to stay in line, Shaggy," Daphne said. "Otherwise, we may not get a Calico Carly."

"How much longer do we have to wait?" asked Shaggy.

"Until the Fowler's red-striped awning opens up," Fred said. "That's the signal the store's about to open."

Somebody's wristwatch alarm started beeping.

"It's nine o'clock!" someone shouted.

Slowly, the red-and-white-striped awning started to unroll. It stretched across the front of the entire store. Just as the awning locked into place with a click, a long yellow banner unfurled from beneath it. The crowd gasped. The front door opened and a man and woman ran out to look at the banner.

"'Beware of Calico Carly,'" the man read. Next to the words was a drawing of a doll with a mean face.

"Zoinks!" Shaggy gasped. "That's the scariest-looking doll I've ever seen!"

"If I didn't know better, I'd say someone's trying to scare everyone away," Velma said.

"Why would someone want to do that?" Daphne asked.

"I don't know," Shaggy moaned. "And I don't want to find out!"

Chapter 2

The man and woman quickly ripped down the banner.

"Don't pay any attention to this, folks," the man said. "Just someone's idea of a bad joke."

"Come on inside, everybody," the woman called. "It's almost time to meet Calico Carly!"

The kids cheered and the crowd slowly started moving through the doors. The man and woman stood outside under the awning, smiling and welcoming people. The gang walked over to them.

"Hi, Mr. and Mrs. Fowler," Fred said.

"Why, hello, Fred," Mrs. Fowler replied with a big smile. "How are you, dear? My, it seems like years since you used to work here."

"You worked here, Fred?" Shaggy said.

"I used to help out in the stockroom after school," Fred explained.

"Excuse me, Mr. Fowler, but we couldn't help but notice the banner," Velma said. "Is everything all right?"

"I certainly hope so," Mr. Fowler answered. "Our store hasn't been doing well ever since the Penny's Worth Toys megastore opened at the mall. So we've put all of our money into selling the new Calico Carly dolls."

"Mr. Fowler's even dressing up in a Calico Carly costume," Mrs. Fowler explained. "If something like this happens again, we may not be able to sell the dolls. We'd go out of business for sure."

"Judging by the crowd, I'd say you should be fine," Velma offered.

"Judging by the crowd, I'd say these people would prefer to have Woofers the Dog," a man said, walking over to them.

"Like, who's Woofers the Dog?" Shaggy asked.

"This is Woofers," the man replied, taking a furry brown toy dog out of a crumpled paper bag. "Say hello, Woofers."

The man pushed a small button on the back of the dog's head. The dog made a slight yipping sound. The man raised the dog to his face and the dog licked his wire-rimmed

glasses. Then the man held Woofers up to Daphne's cheek. The dog stuck out his tongue and gave Daphne a small lick on her cheek.

Scooby-Doo watched Woofers closely. He started growling.

"What's the matter, Scoob?" Shaggy asked with a laugh. "Jealous?"

"Don't worry, Scooby," Daphne said. "It's only a toy."

"See?" the man said. He turned Woofers upside down and opened a small seam in the dog's stomach. He reached in and took out a battery.

"That's a pretty lifelike toy," Velma said.

"Thank you," the man replied, pocketing the battery. "If only you could convince the Fowlers of that."

"What do you mean?" asked Fred.

"This is Claude Frye," Mr. Fowler said. "He's a toy maker. And he's upset that we

11

won't sell Woofers here in the store."

"Times are changing, Claude," Mrs. Fowler said. "Children don't want toy dogs anymore."

"That's because people like you decide to dress up in things like Calico Carly costumes and give out free toys just to sell a doll," Claude complained. "Besides, I don't see why anyone would want a Calico Carly doll when they could have Woofers the Dog. He's cuter, smarter, and just plain better! Come on, Woofers. We know when we're not wanted." Claude Frye took Woofers and walked away angrily.

"Dear, we'd better go inside so you can get ready," Mrs. Fowler said.

"We'll see you kids later," Mr. Fowler said.

"Thanks, Mr. Fowler," Fred said. "Let's go, gang. Into the fun house!"

Chapter 3

The gang walked through the doors and into Fowler's Fun House. They stood just inside the doorway and looked around.

"Jinkies!" Velma exclaimed. "Did you ever see so many different kinds of toys?"

"Don't be fooled, young lady," an older man standing next to her said. He wore a red cardigan sweater and thin wire-rimmed glasses. "There's not as much here as you think."

"They seem to have a pretty good selection," Daphne replied.

"Oh, yeah?" the man said. "Well, they don't have any of these." He opened up a crumpled paper bag and reached inside. He pulled out something and showed it to the gang.

"You're upset because the store doesn't have stubby, wooden, carrot-shaped things?" Shaggy asked.

"It's not a stubby, wooden, carrot thing," the man protested. "It's a wooden top. And it's not just any wooden top, either. It happens to be a Texarkana Twister."

"Rexarrana Rister?" Scooby said.

"One of the fastest, meanest, and strongest tops ever made," the man said.

The man got down on his knees and put down his bag. He wrapped a string around the top. He gave the string a quick yank and

the top took off across the floor.

"That's a Texarkana Twister," the man said proudly. "They don't make 'em like that anymore. And here at Fowler's, they don't sell 'em, either."

"How do you know so much about tops?" Fred asked.

"Sonny Paige is the name, tops are my game," the man said. "I'm the founder and former president of the Downtown Spinners Society. Only trouble is that because of the Fowlers, I had to resign from the club."

"What did the Fowlers do?" Fred asked.

"Stopped selling my tops," Sonny Paige answered. "I used to get all of the club's wooden tops here. Now Butch Bogard gets to be president because he gets our tops on the Internet."

"That's too bad, Mr. Paige," Daphne said.

"I'm not looking for pity," Sonny replied angrily. "I'm looking for justice! Those Fowlers will pay for what they did to me." Sonny Paige grabbed his paper bag and disappeared into the crowd.

"Boy, he sure was angry," Fred said.

"I don't see how anyone can be angry in a place like this," Daphne said, looking around. "It's so full of happy things."

"I'll bet it even took your mind off food, right, Shaggy?" Velma asked. "Shaggy? Scooby?"

Fred, Daphne, and Velma looked around, but there was no sign of Shaggy or Scooby.

Suddenly, they heard a crashing sound from a few aisles away.

"Sounds to me like we found them," Fred said. "Let's go."

Chapter 4

red, Daphne, and Velma ran over and saw that someone had driven a remote-controlled toy car through the side of a cardboard playhouse.

"Shaggy? Scooby?" Daphne called. "Are you all right?"

"Like, we're fine, Daph," Shaggy said from behind her. "But thanks for asking."

"Shaggy!" Daphne exclaimed, turning around. "What are you doing here?"

"Scoob and I went for some food inside the play kitchens," Shaggy answered. "When we got back, we saw you guys running over here."

"If you and Scooby are out here, then who's inside the playhouse?" asked Velma.

A man slowly stepped out from behind the playhouse. He was holding a remote-control box in his right hand. He straightened his eyeglasses and dusted off his jacket.

"Are you all right, sir?" Daphne asked.

"Yes, yes, fine," the man answered. "Completely my fault. I was playing with this radio-controlled car and must have accidentally hit forward instead of reverse."

Just then, Mrs. Fowler came running over.

"Is everything all right?" she said. She saw

the man holding the remote-control unit. "Oh, it's you. Can't you take no for an answer?"

"Terribly sorry, Mrs. Fowler," the man said. He took a business card from his wallet and handed it to her. "Please send a bill to my office. We'll reimburse you for the car and the playhouse. Though I must say I'm surprised you're carrying such low-quality merchandise. You'd never find a cardboard playhouse in one of my stores."

"One of your stores?" asked Daphne.

"Yes, I happen to own a small chain of toy stores," the man said. "Addison Wentworth, chairman and CEO of Penny's Worth Toys."

"He's been itching to buy us out for months," Mrs. Fowler explained. "But Mr. Fowler and I refuse to sell."

"And from what I understand, if your Calico Carly gamble doesn't pay off, you'll have no choice but to sell," Addison Went-

worth said with a smile. "Believe me, Mrs. Fowler, I'm a very patient man."

"Then why don't you go wait someplace else?" said Mrs. Fowler. "You're not welcome in our store."

"If you insist, Mrs. Fowler," replied Addison Wentworth with a small bow. He turned to leave but then he stopped. He opened the remote-control box and took out a battery.

"The battery you left in here was dead,

Mrs. Fowler," Addison Wentworth explained. "Since I like to try out new toys, I always travel with my own batteries. Just in case. Good day, Mrs. Fowler." He slowly walked away, tossing the battery into the air.

"We'll help you straighten up, Mrs. Fowler," Fred said. He and Shaggy lifted up the playhouse as Daphne and Velma moved the car out of the way.

"Thanks, kids," Mrs. Fowler said. "You were a big help. Is there anything I can do for you?"

"Well, Scooby and I were wondering if, like, you had anything other than play food?" Shaggy asked.

"Shaggy, this is a toy store, not a grocery store," Velma said.

"That's all right," said Mrs. Fowler. "It just so happens that we'll be giving out chocolate milk and cookies in a little bit. Think you can wait?"

"Rou ret!" barked Scooby.

"Good. I'll see you at the train station in five minutes," said Mrs. Fowler, smiling, as she turned and walked away.

"Like, why is she going to the train station?" Shaggy asked. "That's clear across town."

"There's an old-fashioned train station set up in the back of the store, by the model trains," Fred explained. "I guess that's where they're going to introduce Calico Carly."

"Well, if they're serving milk and cookies, it sounds like the Fowlers are on the right track," Shaggy replied. Everyone laughed as they walked toward the back of the store.

Chapter 5

S ome of the shoppers were already gathering at the train station. A train whistle blew and Mrs. Fowler came out of the station. She was wearing an engineer's hat.

"Gather 'round, everybody," she called. "The Calico Carly Express has just pulled into Fowler Station. Are you ready to meet Calico Carly?"

Everyone in the crowd cheered.

"I can't hear you!" Mrs. Fowler yelled back. "Are you ready to meet Calico Carly?"

This time, everyone shouted at the top of

their lungs. The train station door flew open and out stepped a life-sized Calico Carly doll. She was dressed in a calico patchwork dress and carried a big calico patchwork bag over her shoulder. Calico Carly waved at the crowd as the children shrieked with happiness.

"Rikes!" Scooby barked as he hid behind Daphne.

"Relax, Scooby, that's only Mr. Fowler wearing a costume," Fred said. "It's not a real doll."

"Welcome, Calico Carly, to Fowler's Fun House," Mrs. Fowler said. "Thank you for making the long trip from Calicoville. I understand that you have a special message for our friends today."

Calico Carly nodded and looked right at the crowd. Then, in a loud, scary voice, Calico Carly yelled, "I warned you to beware of Calico Carly! Now you will pay the price and bear the curse of Calico Carly!" She reached into her big bag and came out with her hands full of tiny toys. She threw them out into the crowd. People immediately started screaming.

"Hey, Calico Carly's throwing toy scorpions and spiders at us!" someone yelled.

"Leave! Leave this place at once!" yelled Calico Carly. "Or the curse of Calico Carly will follow you forever!"

She threw some more rubber bugs into the crowd as people screamed and ran away. Mrs. Fowler looked at Calico Carly.

"Have you lost your mind?" she demanded.

"No, only my head!" Calico Carly exclaimed. The doll took off her head and tossed it to Mrs. Fowler. Mrs. Fowler shrieked and then fainted. The rest of Calico Carly laughed as it ran back through the train station doors.

The gang ran over to Mrs. Fowler.

"Mrs. Fowler, are you all right?" Daphne asked. Fred took the Calico Carly head as Daphne helped Mrs. Fowler to the train station bench.

"I can't believe Mr. Fowler would do something like that," Velma remarked.

"No one's going to want a Calico Carly doll now," Mrs. Fowler said sadly. "It looks like we're going to have to close the store after all."

"Excuse me, Mrs. Fowler, but when did Mr. Fowler start wearing glasses?" asked Fred.

"He doesn't wear glasses," Mrs. Fowler answered. "Why do you ask?"

"Because I don't think Mr. Fowler was wearing the Calico Carly costume," Fred replied. "Look." He reached into the Calico

Carly head and took out a pair of wire-rimmed glasses.

"It looks like whoever was wearing the costume left in such a hurry they forgot their glasses," Velma said.

"But if Mr. Fowler wasn't in the costume, where is he?" Daphne wondered.

"Gang, it looks like we've got a double mystery on our hands," Fred declared. "Don't worry, Mrs. Fowler. We'll look for Mr. Fowler and find out who's behind the toy store terror."

Chapter 6

"I have a hunch that whoever was in the Calico Carly costume isn't going too far without her glasses," Velma stated.

"Velma's right," Fred agreed. "So if we're going to solve this mystery, we'd better get started before Calico Carly comes back for them. That means it's time to split up."

"Shaggy, Scooby, and I will stay here and start looking for clues. We'll keep an eye out for Calico Carly," Velma said.

"Daphne and I will start looking for Mr. Fowler," Fred said.

"And I'll try to calm everybody down," Mrs. Fowler offered. "That is, if anyone's left in the store." She, Fred, and Daphne headed off.

"Shaggy, you and Scooby look around out here," Velma instructed. "I'm going to see if there are any clues on the other side of the train station door." Velma walked through the door, leaving Shaggy and Scooby standing alone at the train station. The head of the Calico Carly costume lay on the floor at the other end of the train platform.

"Man, I don't know about you, Scoob, but that costume head is giving me the creeps," Shaggy said. "Get rid of it, would ya?"

"Rot ree," Scooby said.

"What are you, a scaredy-cat?" Shaggy taunted.

"Meow," Scooby replied.

"I know," Shaggy said. "On the count of three, we'll kick it together. Are you ready,

Scoob? One. Two. Three!"

Just as Shaggy and Scooby ran over to kick the Calico Carly costume head, they heard a roar come from behind the doll display across the aisle. They looked up and saw Calico Carly's body jump up and start walking toward them.

"Don't kick my head!" yelled a voice from inside the costume.

"Zoinks!" Shaggy screamed. "It's, like, the Headless Horseman without the horse!"

Shaggy and Scooby were frozen with fear.

They watched as Calico Carly grabbed her head, put it back on her shoulders, and then ran back behind the dolls.

"I don't know about you, Scooby-Doo," Shaggy said. "But I've got only one thing to say. HELP!"

"What's going on?" Velma asked as she ran back through the train station door. "You two look like you've seen a ghost."

"A doll is more like it," Shaggy responded.

"I'm not surprised," Velma said.

"You're not?" asked Shaggy.

"Of course not, Shaggy," Velma said. "We're in a toy store, remember? Now look at what I found behind the doors." She showed Shaggy and Scooby a crumpled paper bag.

"I found it on the floor next to a pile of little Calico Carly toys," Velma said. "I'll bet that the person in the Calico Carly costume used this bag to hold all those toy spiders and other bugs. Then she dumped them into the Calico Carly bag just before going through the doors. Let's go find Fred and Daphne."

Velma walked off the train platform and headed behind the Calico Carly doll display.

"Oh, no!" Shaggy moaned. "Calico Carly's going to get her for sure! We have to go save Velma!"

Shaggy and Scooby ran over to the display of Calico Carly dolls. Velma was nowhere to be seen. Neither was Calico Carly.

"Velma?" whispered Shaggy. "Velma? Are you okay?"

Scooby sniffed around a little and then shrugged.

"I guess she got away," Shaggy said. He took a close look at one of the dolls. "You know, Scoob, they're not so scary when you see them up close," Shaggy observed. "They're actually kinda cute."

"Gotcha!" Calico Carly yelled as she jumped out from behind the display.

"Zoinks!" exclaimed Shaggy.

"Rikes!" barked Scooby.

"Let's get out of here!" called Shaggy as he and Scooby ran away with Calico Carly close behind them.

Chapter 7

Shaggy and Scooby ran through the store, screaming. Calico Carly was right on their heels. Shaggy and Scooby ran into the stuffed animal department. Shaggy hid behind a giant stuffed gorilla. Scooby dived into a pile of stuffed animals. Only his head poked out. Calico Carly ran right past them.

"Whew!" sighed Shaggy. "Like, that was close. C'mon, Scoob, let's go before Creepy Carly comes back."

When Shaggy and Scooby stood up, they heard the sound of footsteps getting closer.

"Uh-oh," Shaggy groaned. "She's back. Let's hide, quick!" Shaggy pointed to a giant toy chest at the end of one of the aisles. He opened the lid and Mr. Fowler abruptly sat up. His hands were tied behind his back, and a handkerchief covered his mouth.

"Man, what're you doing in there?" Shaggy asked. "Scooby and I need to hide in there from that runaway doll."

The footsteps got louder.

"Oh, no, it's too late!" cried Shaggy. "She's here. We're goners for sure. It's been great knowing you, Scooby-Doo." Shaggy shut his eyes tight. A few moments later, when he opened them, Daphne and Velma were standing in front of him. Fred and Scooby were helping Mr. Fowler out of the toy chest.

"Are you all right, Mr. Fowler?" Fred asked. He untied Mr. Fowler's hands. Mr. Fowler took off the handkerchief.

"I'm fine," he answered. "Thanks to your friends here."

"It was nothing," Shaggy said modestly.

"What happened?" asked Daphne.

"I was in the storeroom getting ready to put on the Calico Carly costume," Mr. Fowler explained.

"The next thing I knew, something hit me on the head. When I woke up, I was tied up inside the toy chest."

"Jeepers," Daphne gasped. "Who could have done that to you?"

"I'm not sure," Mr. Fowler answered. "I never got a good look at her. But I did manage to grab something from her pocket as I fell." He opened his right hand and showed them a small battery.

Fred, Daphne, and Velma looked at one another.

"If you ask me, I think it's time for Calico Carly to get a one-way ticket back to Calicoville," Daphne said.

"Daphne's right," Fred agreed. "Gang, it's time to set a trap. And, Mr. Fowler, we'll need a few supplies."

"Take anything you need, Fred," Mr. Fowler said. "Right now, I'm going to let Mrs. Fowler know I'm all right."

Mr. Fowler went to find his wife. Fred turned to the rest of the gang.

"Okay, here's the plan," Fred said.

"Scooby will wait at the train station for Calico Carly to return. When she shows up,
Scooby will get Calico Carly to chase him
down the main aisle. Shaggy and I will be
waiting to catch Calico Carly."

"Okay, but how do you know Calico
Carly will show up?" asked Daphne.

"Because we still have her glasses," Velma
explained. "I'll bet anything Calico Carly will
show up to look for them — and to scare
Scooby."

"Rulp," Scooby said.

"Daphne, you and Velma get
two jump ropes and a pair of
in-line skates,"
instructed Fred.

"Sounds like a good
plan, Fred," Shaggy
said. "There are only two
things you forgot to leave
out."

"What are they?" asked Fred.

"Me and Scooby," Shaggy replied.

Scooby-Doo nodded in agreement.

"Won't you help us, Scooby?" asked Daphne. "There's still a whole bunch of chocolate milk and cookies that haven't been eaten."

"Ruh-uh," Scooby said, shaking his head.

"Believe me, it'll take more than some milk and cookies to get Scooby to change his mind," Shaggy declared.

"How about a Scooby Snack, too?" Velma offered.

"Rokay!" barked Scooby. He jumped up and gobbled down the snack that Velma tossed into the air.

"Now that that's been settled," Fred said, "let's get to work!"

Chapter 8

F red, Shaggy, and Scooby stood at the train station inside Fowler's Fun House. Velma and Daphne soon came over with the supplies Fred had requested.

"Here, Scooby, I'll help you put on your skates," Daphne said.

"And look," Velma said. "We even got you some safety equipment."

While Daphne tied on the skates, Velma clipped a helmet on Scooby's head. Then she strapped on some elbow and knee pads.

"Like, it's Skating Scooby, ready for action!" Shaggy joked. He helped Scooby stand up. Scooby lost his balance and his feet went flying out from under him. He landed on his tail with a thud.

"Rouch!" barked Scooby.

"Maybe you should have gotten a tail pad, too, Velma," Shaggy joked.

"Here are the jump ropes, Fred," Daphne said, handing them to him.

"Thanks," Fred said. "Shaggy, you and I will take these and wait for Calico Carly at the end of that aisle. Places, everyone."

But before anyone could move, Calico Carly burst through the train station door.

"I warned all of you to leave this store!" the doll screamed at them. "Now you shall all be punished!" She let out a shriek.

"Zoinks!" yelled Shaggy. "What do we do now, Fred?"

"Run!" shouted Fred.

Fred, Daphne, Velma, and Shaggy each ran in a different direction. Scooby tried to

stand up, but he kept slipping on the skates. Finally, using his tail for extra balance, he managed to get back up. Calico Carly reached out to grab him. But Scooby ducked and pushed himself backward off Calico Carly's stomach.

Scooby rolled backward off the train platform and onto the slick floor of the toy store. He started picking up speed as he watched Calico Carly run toward him.

"Rikes!" barked Scooby. He grabbed hold of a giant teddy bear and managed to turn himself around. Scooby skated faster and faster down the main aisle of the toy store.

Calico Carly grabbed a skateboard from one of the displays and started after him.

"Relp! Raggy!" shouted Scooby.

"Back here!" Shaggy called back.

Scooby turned his head in the direction of Shaggy's voice.

"Head for the back of the store!" Shaggy called.

When he turned to face forward, Scooby saw he was heading right for a trampoline that was resting on its side.

"Ruh-roh!" Scooby said.

Scooby skated right into the trampoline and bounced off. He rocketed past Calico Carly, who fell off the skateboard. But the giant doll soon found a scooter and took off after Scooby again.

Calico Carly closed in on Scooby, who was starting to slow down. Suddenly, Scooby skated over one of the little toy spiders. It got caught in his wheels, stopping the skates.

Scooby fell over and slid across the floor. Calico Carly swerved out of the way and crashed right into the giant Calico Carly doll display.

Daphne and Velma ran over to help Scooby-Doo. The Fowlers came running down the aisle as Fred and Shaggy wrapped the jump ropes around Calico Carly.

"Now let's see who's been the cause of all this commotion," Mr. Fowler said.

Chapter 9

M r. Fowler reached over and pulled off Calico Carly's head.

"Claude Frye!" Mr. Fowler exclaimed. "You?"

"Just as we suspected," Velma said.

"My goodness, how did you know?" Mrs. Fowler asked.

"Well, to be honest, we weren't sure at first," Daphne admitted. "After all, there were three people who all had reasons for wanting the store to fail."

"And the first clue we found confirmed

that any of them could've been in the costume," Velma continued. "Claude Frye, Sonny Paige, and Addison Wentworth all wear the kind of eyeglasses we found."

"It wasn't until we put the other clues together that we were able to figure out the real culprit," said Fred.

"When we found the crumpled paper bag in the back of the train station, it reminded us of the one Claude Frye kept Woofers in," said Velma.

"But it also looked like the one Sonny Paige carried his tops in," added Daphne. "It wasn't until Mr. Fowler showed us the battery that we realized it was Mr. Frye."

"But didn't Addison Wentworth take a battery out of the remote-control box before he left?" asked Mrs. Fowler.

"Yes, but only Mr. Frye could have left all three clues," Fred explained. "He wears glasses, carried a crumpled shopping bag, and had a battery in his pocket. Besides, he's also the only one who knew that Calico Carly was going to be giving out toys to the children."

"He mentioned it when we were talking to him outside, remember?" Velma said.

"How long were you planning this, Claude?" demanded Mr. Fowler.

"For weeks, ever since you turned me and Woofers away," said Claude Frye, scowling. "Toys like Calico Carly and those buzzing and flashing electronic doodads are making it harder and harder for me to sell my own toys.

So I decided to take revenge on those mass-produced toys. Once word spread about the curse of Calico Carly, toy stores everywhere would stop carrying it and want to sell nice toys, like my Woofers. And my plan would have worked, too. Except those kids and their real-life meddling mutt got in my way."

"Kids, how can we thank you?" Mr. Fowler asked.

"And more important, how can we get our customers back?" Mrs. Fowler added.

"I have an idea that should answer both questions," Fred said. He whispered something to Mr. Fowler.

"Sounds good to me!" Mr. Fowler replied. "Claude, I have a proposition for you." Mr. Fowler knelt down and whispered something to Claude Frye.

"I'll do it!" exclaimed Claude Frye. "Untie me and I'll get right to work."

"You can use my workroom in the back,"

Mr. Fowler offered. "Just come with me."

"I'll join you," Fred said. He followed Claude Frye to the back of the store.

Mrs. Fowler brought over some chocolate milk and cookies for everyone. A little while later, Claude Frye returned with Fred. This time, Claude carried a cardboard box.

"Ladies and gentlemen, introducing the newest addition to Fowler's Fun House," Claude Frye said as he reached into the box and took out a toy dog with Scooby's face. "Scooby-Doo, the Mystery-Solving Dog!"

"Hey, like, that's you, Scooby-Doo!" Shaggy exclaimed.

"Actually, it's Scooby's face on Woofer's body," Claude explained. "But we can fix that later."

"What do you think, Mr. Fowler?" asked Fred.

"I'm not the one you should be asking," answered Mr. Fowler. "How about you, Scooby?"

Scooby looked at the dog carefully. He leaned over and sniffed the toy's nose. Claude pushed a button on the back of the dog's head. The dog licked Scooby and then barked.

"Scooby-Dooby-Doo!" it said.

Scooby smiled. Everyone laughed as Scooby gave the toy dog a great big lick in return.

About the Author

As a boy, James Gelsey used to run home from school to watch the Scooby-Doo cartoons on television (only after finishing his homework). Today, he still enjoys watching them with his wife and two daughters. He also has a real dog named Scooby who loves nothing more than a good Scooby Snack!

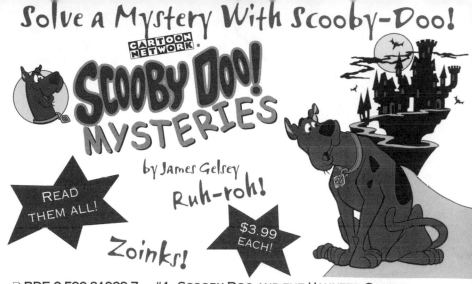